An Awakening Within

A Novel and Spiritual Journey
By Joseph Mattioli

Contact with author may be made by writing to Mattioli Enterprises 11997 Cadillac Drive, Suite 102, Independence, KY 41051.

Printed in Victoria, Canada.

Front Cover Picture, istockphoto #29390
Copyright Daniel Norman.
Printed with Permission.

National Library of Canada Cataloguing in Publication Data

```
Mattioli, Joseph, 1947-
      An awakening within / Joseph Mattioli.
ISBN 1-4120-0417-9
      I. Title.
PS3613 A858 A93 2003          813'.6      C2003-903086-5
```

TRAFFORD

This book was published *on-demand* in cooperation with Trafford Publishing. On-demand publishing is a unique process and service of making a book available for retail sale to the public taking advantage of on-demand manufacturing and Internet marketing. **On-demand publishing** includes promotions, retail sales, manufacturing, order fulfilment, accounting and collecting royalties on behalf of the author.

Suite 6E, 2333 Government St., Victoria, B.C. V8T 4P4, CANADA
Phone 250-383-6864 Toll-free 1-888-232-4444 (Canada & US)
Fax 250-383-6804 E-mail sales@trafford.com
Web site www.trafford.com TRAFFORD PUBLISHING IS A DIVISION OF TRAFFORD HOLDINGS LTD.
Trafford Catalogue #03-0786 www.trafford.com/robots/03-0786.html

10 9 8 7 6 5 4 3 2

Table of Contents

Introduction

by Reader

Each life has its own story. Part of that story is the spiritual journey each one of us takes. It is a journey of faith in the unseen; a search for the sacred; the pursuit of the true, the good and the beautiful; and, the ultimate questions about life and death. Though it is a universal journey, it is one without universal agreement.

In this short but powerful book, Joe Mattioli shares a story of one person on a search for answers to those important questions. Like most of us, the main character in the story, is living what he thinks is the good life. The good life that he, and most of us, believe in because of what we have learned from others. But a casual trip to the Holy Land with a local church group turns into a surprisingly profound spiritual experience. Amid the heat, sand, rocks, and air of an ancient land comes strange events that change a life forever.

Like all of us, new things do not come easily and without reconciliation with the old. It is not an easy struggle. But it is one that in the end brings a peace and a faith never known before. The teachings of Jesus take on a new vitality and richness gleaned only as it can through the searching spirit. It is an experience that both challenges and deepens long-held cherished Christian beliefs. It is an experience that only the individual spirit can partake with all its fears and hopes. It is an experience that can happen only with a living God and an open spirit.

It is not a book that has all the answers, nor does it try to be. It is the story of the spiritual journey of one person, yet it is the story of us all. For it is much as T.S. Eliot once said, that at the end of all our exploring we shall come back to where we started and know it for the first time. And if this book does anything, it may help do just that.

Chapter 1
The Good News

The year was 1988. It was a remarkable year for me. Prosperity was at my door. Everything I touched seemed to turn to gold. As a software programmer for the General Electric Company, I was getting paid well to have what I considered fun. There was great satisfaction in the tasks I was assigned and my dabbling in the stock market was very favorable to my pocketbook. My criteria for happiness was narrow as my life existed primarily in my work. I was sheltered from most of life's storms and content. What more could I ask of life?

It all started on a Sunday in October while attending morning service at a small Baptist church in Cincinnati, Ohio. There was nothing special about this particular church that would make it stand out. It was your typical congregation of pleasant and friendly church people. Little did I know that something was about to happen that day. How could I know that my life was about to change forever.

The church was beautifully decorated and arrayed in colors of red, blue and purple. The pastor stood behind a massive oak lectern. His voice was amplified by an expensive deep base audio system and his black attire gave his words a real sense of authority. The message was the same as always but there was an unexplainable feeling within me that said today was going to be a starting point that would alter the rest of my life. At the end of the service, the pastor announced that for part of December he would not be present since he was going to the Holy Land with a small group that had signed up for the trip months ago. I always wanted to go to the Holy Land but never got past the thinking about it part. I wondered to myself how I had missed his past announcement and the sign up invitation. Then I remembered that most of the time, in church, I was busy day-dreaming while the pastor was talking. Somehow I enjoyed sitting in church among the people with my silent thoughts living fantasies while others listened intently as if something new was being said.

As the service ended, I started towards the door only to find that the pastor had arrived there before me. Pastor Jenkins was now shaking hands with those leaving. Impatiently, I slowly moved along near the end of the line of people. I now wished that I had taken a seat in the back of the church as I usually do. This would have allowed me to escape the exiting ritual that was so commonplace here. A brief handshake and a thank you were the price I would pay to get out of the door. I had hoped to escape this ritual but this day it was not meant to be.

I had taken a third row seat that day so I could get a better look at Judy Schreiber, a young unmarried girl, who always sat in the second row. She always wore a perfume that reminded me of fresh tulips from a botanical garden I went to as a boy with my parents. We had never talked before as I was too shy to strike up a conversation. Somehow I thought she was too good for me. However, that didn't stop me from thinking about her and fixing my eyes on her voluptuous figure as I heard the sermon as a distant drum in the background while daydreaming things I dare not speak of in church.

Finally, the pastor reached out his hand to shake mine but instead of the usual "Hello Joe, glad to see you today" and "See you next week", he said, "Joe, could you stay around a few minutes, I have something I want to talk to you about." My curiosity got the best of me, and rather than making an excuse, I said "sure, I'll wait by your office." "No. Go in and wait. I'll be right there," he said.

I went into his small office located at the front of church. I helped myself to a seat on his couch to the side of the desk. From there I could see him at the front door finishing up his good-byes as I wondered what all this could be about. My eyes caught a group of many of his diplomas on the wall. One said ORDINATION in capital letters and another said DOCTORATE DEGREE. Pastor Jenkins must have had a lot of education because there were two more diplomas on the wall that I couldn't quite read from where I sat. I had talked to him before but had never been invited into his office.

As I waited, I recalled his sermon a month ago on the Bible. He had preached on how we ought to read it every day to get to know Jesus Christ better. He said the Bible was the final authority in his church and in any other Christian church that followed God. I had cornered him before the next service the week following because I could not understand how our Bible could be a final authority as it seemed every religion had its own book written by men that claimed the same thing. Somewhere in it I remembered reading that God was a living God. I struggled to understand why a living God would require us to get our instruction from a book rather than directly from him. Was he limited in that he could be at only one place at a time? Pastor Jenkins was kind enough to take me aside and explain that this book we called the Bible had survived for more than a thousand years and through the dark ages as proof that God's hand was in it. He explained the words in it were God's instructions to us. It was God's plan that we put our trust or faith as he called it in this Book. He explained that we were to follow this Book until we died. If we lived as the Book said, then when we died we would go to be with God in heaven and we would understand all of this more clearly. I was amazed at how easily he had answered my question. He must have had a lot of schooling and studying to have so much insight and be able to answer so quickly, I thought. Just then he entered his office.

"Joe", he said, "there has been a cancellation by Mrs. Petula for the Holy Land trip and she has agreed to forfeit her 20 % deposit to someone else who might want to go. I thought perhaps that you might be interested."

What ever gave him that thought I don't know but I answered "yes I was interested." "Would there be time for me to get a passport?" I asked.

"If you go first thing Monday, I am told it will be ready in December about 3 days before we leave." He responded.

Without hesitation, I said "sure, I'd love to". He summarized the itinerary into 5 minutes and then off I sped with a load of paperwork containing release forms and instructions on how to pack, what to bring and an itinerary of the whole 13 day excursion. How fortunate, I thought. Not only did I want to go but also I was going for 20% less than everyone else.

God, I loved bargains!

I took a personal day off Monday to start the passport process. After spending the morning across the river at the Covington Post Office filling out paperwork and returning later with a small 2" by 2" photo and the proper fees I felt relieved. These things sometimes take more time than expected and I was glad to get it out of the way. I did this not even considering if my boss would give me any vacation time with so short a notice for the trip. That was definitely not the usual me. Something new was happening and I was surprised at how quickly I had gone forward without more consideration.

The next Tuesday, I went in to talk to my boss Richard. I anticipated that he would give me a hard time. Being a large company, GE usually required notice of vacation 6 months in advance for planning purposes. Richard explained vacation policy to me and reminded me of the need to complete the latest software project he had assigned me. He reminded me it had to be completed on schedule. I agreed to work on weekends and without extra pay and provide a daily progress sheet if he would approve the time off. Reluctantly, he agreed after he tired of my reminding him of my past record of completion of projects. I got the idea he really didn't care about the past. He was more concerned about the future and rumors of potential lay-off. Anyway, he agreed on the condition that my portion of the project was completed first.

The time passed quickly as I pushed myself to complete and test the software code three weeks before schedule. I was amazed, as what could be accomplished in such a short time when there was an incentive to do so. I recalled the time in the seventh grade when my Dad offered me ten dollars if I would get straight A's on my next report card. I had never even come close before but in the 50's, ten dollars was a lot of money for a twelve-year-old. Well, I did it and he never offered me money like that again and I never made straight A's again either.

I was raised a Catholic like the rest of our Italian family. After a long absence from the Catholic Church, I needed something different. What I needed I did not know at the time. Although I considered myself happy and had no problem with depression, I somehow sensed that something was missing. So a couple of years ago I had joined this Baptist church and that's why I shortly would be on my way to the Holy Land. They called it the Holy Land but somehow I could not understand how one piece of ground could be any holier than another is.

It was December, a week before the trip, I got a letter confirming all the arrangements and the list of people who would be traveling in our group. Boy, was I shocked to see that Judy Schreiber was on the list. I never even considered checking into who was going. I was too busy working and caught up in thoughts of what kind of strange adventure I was about to go on. Here I was in my 40's and never married except to my job. I had never been out of the United States before and travel was only a thing I had been content to dream about all my life.

Chapter 2
The Trip to Israel

The day finally arrived. The weather was cloudy and cold with snow expected shortly. I left my car at the church and rode to the airport in the church bus. Traffic was particularly heavy as it was 7:00 AM rush hour. I wasn't sitting close to Judy but I could still smell that fragrance that was so distinctively hers. We spent a long time getting organized and checking through the airport. After more than the usual processing time, we finally boarded.

I sat between two older women who I assumed probably traveled much of their life. They seemed so at ease and not the least bit excited about the plane ride. After a couple hours after our stop and change in New York they were both of them fast asleep and snoring. It was to be such a long trip. Never before had I been on a plane for 13 hours. I must have read the magazines on the plane five times over and my mind was too busy to sleep as others did. A movie helped to pass the time but brought no sleep for me.

When we arrived in Israel the day was just getting started. I was suffering from lack of sleep and jet lag. It would be several days of touring and sleeping before I felt somewhat back to my normal self.

I must admit I was a bit puzzled concerning the locals here. Christianity seemed locally almost non-existent except for tourists. How can this be I thought. Here we have a place where Christianity had its roots and now the dominant people are Moslems and Jews. They were here cashing in on our visit but having no part of our belief. I guess I should have known it. I just never paid much attention in world history class as daydreaming was my favorite pastime.

We visited Bethlehem, the Sea of Galilee and the place where the Sermon on the Mount was believed to have been delivered. We ate Saint Peter fish from the sea, visited the upper room where the Holy Spirit was believed to have been given to the apostles, visited the village of Caesarea and of course the Garden of Gethsemane. We walked the Wailing Wall and the Stations of the Cross. The story of the Bible was trying to come alive before me but I was highly distracted by all the commercialism. Everywhere there were vendors selling trinkets, souvenirs, and crosses and dressed up places of biblical significance to be seen. We stayed in 5 star hotels and ate the best of foods. Time seemed to fly by until the end of the week when we were to go to Egypt. That is where my real journey began...

Chapter 3
The Road to Egypt

This day we were to head for a 2-day excursion to Egypt. Our itinerary included seeing the pyramids, taking pictures and camel rides. We would arrive in Cairo in time for supper. The road was paved and from the look of traffic and condition seemed hardly traveled. We were to travel by bus across this desert. It was a route that was of the same terrain that the Hebrews traveled when they left Egypt for Mount Sinai and the Promised Land. Our guides were Muslims and spoke among themselves in a language we could not understand. We were boarded by 10:00 A.M. Moments after we started on our way.

There were no restaurants on this road. We didn't even see a village. For endless miles and miles just sand and rock and desert filled the landscape. Our guides had packed a bag lunch for us. We were to eat supper at a 5 star hotel in Egypt. After several hours and some history lessons they served us lunch. It was some sort of baked chicken and very poorly cooked. After only a few bites, I tossed it in disgust back in the bag and ate the banana that was included with the chicken and a bottle of water. Shortly after that time we resumed our history lesson from our guide Zechariah but were distracted by the sputtering sound of our bus engine, which in future moments found complete silence.

Anxiety, was soon prevalent among us Christians. It was a modern reliving of the Exodus through the desert. People were whining and complaining. "How will we get out of here? Lunch was bad and we are still hungry. How long will it be before help comes?" The air conditioning was now out and the temperature was rising quickly. Even with windows open it was suffocatingly hot. Everyone was complaining as if these minor inconveniences were life threatening. Many remarked how they wished they had never come. Oh how spoiled we are by modern conveniences, I thought. "Where would we get water when our lunch drink was finished?" Some asked. Strangely, there were no answers given to these questions as our guides didn't seem troubled as they talked among themselves and focused their attention under the hood of the bus.

It grew swelteringly hot in the bus. The whining was so irritating to my spirit that I stepped out of the bus and walked unnoticed toward a small group of room sized boulders about a hundred yards off the left side of the road. They were stacked one upon another which I judged to be 2-3 stories high. There was shade to be had there. I arrived and took a seat on a smaller rock shaded by the larger boulders. I noticed it was still hot. I imagined it was in the low 100's. But it was so much more peaceful than it was on the bus. I thought to myself that I should go back and tell Judy about this place. It would give me a chance to strike up a conversation while we waited for help to come or the guides to fix whatever was wrong. But I was so pleasantly at peace that my thoughts soon drifted away.

I noticed out of the corner of my eye a dark crevice in the boulder next to me. It almost looked wide enough to pass through. It couldn't go far as the whole group of boulders was no bigger than a small 2-story house. Curiosity got the better of me and I took another look at the bus and noticed more people getting off and standing and sitting on the shaded side along the hot pavement. I guessed we were going to be here for a while. So I slipped sideways through the thin crevice losing sight of the outside world. As I passed on the inside of the boulder, I was surprised to find I was in a room of sorts where boulders made up the walls and ceiling. There was just enough light entering from the edges of boulders making up the roof to see clearly. Here I was standing on a sandy floor with boulders around me and one extremely large boulder above me.

It was surprisingly cool inside. So much so that it felt air-conditioned. I followed each line where the boulders joined and saw no other entrance or exit other than where I had entered. There were no drawings or painting on the rocks. I could not understand how something like this that had been around for so long would not have graffiti on the inside. I could see that the footprints where I had walked were the only indention in the sand of the room. How could this be that a formation such as this so close to the only road had not been discovered or graced by graffiti by now? I wondered.

I looked for bugs on the ground and any other kind of life form before I sat in an Indian position on the sandy floor in the middle of this cool and strange enclosure. I found nothing. The guides had not mentioned anything like this in the middle of the desert. The one guide had only said that it gets cold at night in the desert so I reasoned somehow these rocks must store the cool air and the heat to find an average temperature that is very comfortable. The walls were naturally smooth and bulged in toward the center of the room. I wondered how they could have come into being in this arrangement.

Each of the four walls was practically identical in tan color and grainy texture. I examined them over and over with my eyes trying to make images like one does with the clouds. They were plain and contained no interesting features. Except for the narrow slit where I entered and the slits between the rocks that let in a small amount of light, it was a room of nothingness. As I sat there, amazed or rather astonished at finding this, I suddenly felt panic overcome me. Thoughts that the bus might have left without me surfaced in my mind. I quickly sprang to my feet and headed for the narrow opening in the rocks. In the process of my haste I scraped my arms trying to navigate the slit so quickly. I paused and noticed my arm had surface skin abrasions but I quickly turned my attention around the rock to where the bus was, only to have my worst fear realized.

The bus was gone! How could no one notice that I was not aboard? How could I not have heard it? Didn't anyone see me walking toward the rocks? Didn't the guides take a head count before leaving? Panic again gripped me as I ran to the place where the bus was. I was hoping that somehow it would magically be there when I arrived. But it was not to be. All I could see was black pavement in both directions as far as the eye could see. Surely, another bus from another tour or someone would be along? Or surely they would miss me and come back? My mind was in a panic. What was I to do? I was calm before when the rest of the people were whining, but now it was my turn to complain.

After staring at what seemed endlessly in both directions, I felt light-headed and faint. How long had I been standing in this extreme heat? I knew I must get out of the sun fast. I drew a large SOS in the sand with my shoe and an arrow pointing to the rocks. Reluctantly, I headed back to the rock formation where I could get cool and think straight.

Chapter 4
A Strange Encounter

As I re-entered the formation, more carefully than I had exited, I noticed the abrasions on my arms from my quick exit were gone. This struck me odd but I had greater concerns to ponder. Maybe, I did no damage after all. I realized for the first time I was thirsty. I approached the middle of the cool room and sat down as before and felt suddenly at peace and forgot about my thirst.

As the afternoon faded, the light inside the room slowly grew dimmer. I knew night was fast approaching. Maybe it would be cooler outside and I could see approaching vehicle lights on the horizon. I went back out and noticed the temperature had dropped dramatically but still I saw not a sign of anyone for what seemed like hours. A rising moon in a starry sky were the only lights to be seen. Finally, it got too cold for me and I decided I had better return to the rock room for the night rather than suffer from my lack of covering in the cold.

Sure enough it was warmer inside. The rocks were now giving off the warmth they had stored up all day under the blistering heat. I could not see well now. Only a small amount of moonlight entered through the slits of the rocks. Exhausted from my thoughts I somehow dozed off only to be awakened shortly by a voice that echoed within the room. “Do not be afraid,” the voice said as if it were a command. I gathered my composure and strained to see who was inside this formation with me. I looked around but I saw no one. Maybe, I am hearing things, I thought. Then I remembered reading in the Bible where Samuel was a boy and one night the Lord spoke to him. He thought it was his master Eli. He then went to Eli and asked what he wanted. Eli said he had not called but finally figured that it was God talking to Samuel and he told him the next time he heard the voice to answer.

I decided not to wait for the voice again and instead I asked as if expecting an answer. “Who is it that is speaking to me?” Clearly and succinctly I heard a voice saying, “It is I Jesus of Nazareth that is speaking.” I did not believe it but I certainly heard the voice as my body went into shock. I couldn’t move or speak for what seemed like minutes. My strength was gone out of me and I was frightened beyond measure. I finally mustered enough strength to shakily say with tears in my eyes, “Help me, I am afraid”. To which an answer was forth-coming saying, "What are you afraid of?" "That which I cannot see, I am afraid of." I responded.

Gradually the formation of rocks took on a mellow glow as if reflecting a light I could not see. Before me appeared a man of normal statue, neither handsome that he should stand out nor intimidating that I should fear. He spoke again and said "Why are you yet afraid?" I answered. "Even though I see now I still am afraid of that which I do not understand. If you are Jesus then why don't you look like any of your pictures?"

Calmly he spoke. "How should I look? And where did you get your pictures of me?" Not waiting for an answer he continued. "In my day, we had no cameras and there was nothing about my looks that an artist would desire to draw."

Not really believing it was he but speaking as if I did, I said. "But there are churches filled with beautiful pictures of you. People have put you on windows and book covers. You are attached to crosses and even with the thorns on your head as a crown you are pictured with wonderful features of beauty. I pictured you taller and one that would stand out in a crowd." I said indifferently. My fear was gone as I wrapped my thoughts in my words.

To which this man who identified himself as Jesus

said. “You certainly do err in your thoughts. Have you not read in the Book you call the Bible, in the book of Isaiah, “He had no form nor comeliness that we should desire him?” Does it not say “We esteemed him not and that I was despised and rejected of men?” In your New Testament gospels doesn’t it say that I escaped from my enemies among the crowds many times? Do you think that this fits your descriptions from your pictures?”

“No, I guess not”, I reluctantly admitted. “I guess we tend to use our imagination a lot in our society. I don‘t think the people who made the drawings meant any harm by their inaccurate portrayal. But why do I not see the marks on your head and hands now?” I continued.

“As a Christian, you profess to believe in your Bible. Why have you not even examined it closely for an answer to this question before you ask?” He said.

“What do you mean?” I responded. How could I possibly know the answer to this question and how does he know I am a Christian and profess to believe in the Bible? I asked of myself defensively.

“If you will recall in the gospels, after I was put to death, I appeared to my disciples many times. On more than one occasion they did not recognize me. In fact in the Gospel according to Luke in your

Chapter 24 it was recorded that I appeared to two of my disciples on their way to a village called Emmaus. I talked to them as we walked together for some time yet they recognized me not until their eyes were opened. If I were limited to one flesh, don't you think they would have surely recognized me when they first saw me close? If I was given power to lay down this flesh, and take it up again, do you think I am now limited to a particular look or body form?" He spoke softly.

I knew what he said was true but I could only say, "I guess so". How stupid of me I thought. Who am I kidding? If this is Jesus, then let me not waste time on such foolish questions. There have to be more important things I want to know. But it was not to be for awhile. All I could think of were trivial questions until I at last asked something profound. "Are you God?" I asked in all sincerity.

"What makes you think that?" He answered my question with a question. "Well," I said, "There has been a lot of confusion in your churches concerning this. Most say you are God made flesh; a few say you were a great prophet; some say you were a son of God; others say you are a servant of God and still others just don't know. All of them read parts of the same book but come to different conclusions."

"Throughout time there have been many people who

have been made a God by their followers. An important question to ask from the start is "What is that person's own testimony concerning this question?" In other words, what is recorded of me saying of myself? In your book you call the New Testament, you have the words that I am believed to have spoken printed in red. If I were God would I not have said so plainly or would I have lied or tried to deceive you? It is recorded in red letters that I said I am the Son of Man. It is recorded I acknowledged I was the Christ that was prophesied to come. It is recorded I called God my Father and therein I testified I was his Son. It is recorded that I said God sent me but it is not recorded that I ever said I was God. Are we not all God's children? And in truth, my life was my testament and witness, not the words in a book. God lived in me but you can not limit God to a man", he spoke in a soft voice.

"But it was also recorded you said that you and your Father were one", I retorted as if to argue the point.

"Yes, and do you know what that means?" He answered.

"Well, I know what I was taught that it meant but now I am less certain. Will you explain it to me please?" I asked almost apologetically.

"First of all if you read down 5 versus you would see

that I said "Do I blaspheme because I said I am the Son of God?" Nevertheless, I will explain what was meant by that which appears as I and my Father are one. I told my disciples that the words that I spoke were not my own words but that which I heard the Father say. I didn't do my own works but that which he showed me. I did the will of the Father during my ministry. In that I chose to make his will and my will the same, I was one with him or as you would say in agreement with his desire. That is what it means to be one with the Father. There was a time you have recorded in the garden before I laid down my life where I had a struggle and my will was different from His but after much fervent prayer, I said "Nevertheless, your will be done." In your Gospel of John it is recorded that I prayed to the Father that my disciples should be one even as I was one with the Father. It is then recorded that I was asking not only for them but for all that should believe. Now if that meant that I was saying that I was God, then why wouldn't it also be saying that all who believe and do the Father's will are one and therefore make them God also?" He asked looking for my response.

After some thought I answered "Yes, I imagine it would. I just never thought of it that way. It makes very little sense to interpret those words as saying you were God if we also could be one with the Father by believing", I added. Then I thought of another thing I remembered reading and said. "It is true that you are not recorded saying you were God but it is recorded that you once said that if you have seen me then you have seen the Father or something like that"

"It is recorded in your gospel of John that I said if you had seen me then you have seen the Father. One must remember that God is a spirit. This I taught to all that listened to my words. It is also recorded that no man at any time has seen God. God cannot be seen with eyes of the flesh. But those who saw me do the works of the Father have in the flesh in as much as possible with their eyes seen the works of the Father. In a sense they have perceived the presence of the Father. If you yet do not believe, you can examine this further. In the language of the book of John, which was written in Greek, the word for seen used in this reference was "*horao*" that is a non-casual vision or perception. It is not used for something that is casually seen which would use the Greek word "*eido*". "*Horao*" was used instead in the past tense because it is not a casual seeing but rather a perception or discernment of the Father in me because I did his works. Do you understand what I am saying?" He asked.

"Yes... I believe I do. You are saying that there are multiple words that can be translated to the word "seen". In this case the word in the original Greek is not a literal seeing such as an image equals an image but rather as an image is like an image by perception. Being a software programmer, I use the concept often in my program code to modify a fixed element without changing the original. Kind of like when I was in a high school play acting out the part of an Englishman. I was **seen** as that person cause I was saying and doing as that person would be but I was not actually that person. I was just representing him", I said slowly but with confidence.

"That would be a fair analogy of what I meant" he said approvingly. "To believe that when my disciples literally saw me that they saw God would make no sense. God is not a man and therefore cannot be confined to one man or one location."

Just then I thought of another writing I had always had a problem with concerning this belief. "Somewhere it was recorded that you said that before Abraham was you existed. You even said verily, verily before those words. I was always taught that when you said those words that it meant truly, truly, which meant it was very definitely so. That would surely seem to be saying that you existed before him yet you came here after him. Doesn't that imply that you were God?" I said.

"It is your John 58:8 you refer to. You must also read the 2 sentences you call versus before that verse. Many of the Jews of my time wanted to trap me in words. They tried this by asking me if I was greater than their father Abraham, whom was dead. I told them that he rejoiced to see my day. No doubt they interpreted that as me saying that my flesh was there with him. Abraham was the receiver of the promise for all his children and God showed him what was to come. He saw my day by the spirit of prophecy and rejoiced by faith. In this he was justified and so by faith received the promise then that was to come by me. The Jews present then said or asked rather sarcastically. You are not yet 50 years old and you have seen Abraham? They asked as a question but it was not one they expected an answer from. First of all they erred in thinking that Abraham was dead. God is not the God of the dead but of the living. Abraham indeed lives even today as I do. Of course, my flesh was not yet 50 years old and my flesh had not seen Abraham but he had seen my day by faith and rejoiced in it. And then as the Father spoke in my ear I spoke as his oracle and said most assuredly, or as you say verily, verily, before or prior to the flesh you know as Abraham came to this earth, I existed. I was speaking of the spirit and not of the flesh."

"Even in the book you call the Old Testament it was written that man was created on the sixth day or age. He was created in the image of God as a living spirit. There is no record of man being created after that. We all come from God and God was there in the beginning before the flesh you know as Abraham existed. The anointing of God which is the Spirit of God in man or the Christ of God was speaking truth. It is that which is in communion with the Father, which I by faith manifested to all men. Seeing that they were blinded to the truth they still didn't understand and instead desired to stone me."

After a brief pause he continued. "If I were God and overcame this world, it would prove nothing. God cannot be tempted. But if I was a man as you are and tempted in all ways and yielding to the Spirit of God overcame the world, then there is hope for you."

Continuing he said. "You were also made in the likeness of God. If this anointing of God or Christ that was in me was only there because I was God, then what is your hope? Overcoming the world on my part would have been a sure thing and proven nothing. But since I was not God but rather a son as you, you now have that same hope. God sent and was with many men recorded in your Bible but that doesn't make them God"

For the past few minutes I had forgotten where I was. I remembered that I had been thirsty but for some reason my thirst was now gone. I looked away from the figure before me and when my eyes returned, I was alone. Was this a dream? I pinched myself and I felt pain. The walls were still here and

I decided to head back through the narrow opening in the rocks.

I headed to the road and again focused my eyes on the dark road that was straight and disappeared in the darkness. I heard not a sound nor did I see lights of any kind. I was quickly getting cold again and decided to head back to the formation of rocks. What a story I would have when morning came and some vehicle picked me up, I thought. The road was in great repair and assuredly there must be more traffic during the day although I couldn't recall seeing others pass by the day before.

Again entering the the rock formation, I sat down in the center of the room where the temperature was once again comfortable. I was tired. I slowly closed my eyes and rested.

Chapter 5
A Second Encounter

How long my eyes were shut I do not know. There was no sound to be heard. Yet my eyes opened as if it were morning. Still, there was nothing to be seen. Finally, I mustered the courage to speak out loud and said, "Jesus, will you come back to talk with me?" No sooner had I asked when the walls again took on a familiar glow and before me stood this selfsame man as I had seen before. I wanted so desperately to ask the right questions. It is so easy to think of what to ask when there is no one to answer, but now I knew not what to say first. Finally, I opened my mouth and asked. "Why did you leave your words in the New Testament Bible for us when it seems to cause so many divisions in your followers?"

He answered slowly and deliberately, "What makes you think I intended to leave any writings for you?" Not waiting for an answer, he continued. "I commanded my disciples to go into the entire world and preach the Gospel. I did not command them to write any books with the exception of the book of prophecy, which you know as the Apocalypse or book of Revelations. I told them to go among the people and speak that which they heard in their ears. I told them not to think of what they were to say but that God would speak to them in that selfsame hour what to say."

"You mean even your own disciples did other than they were instructed to do? And if so, why?" I asked confused.

"My disciples were men as you. It is in the nature of men to record things. The letters that they wrote were never meant by them to become part of a book that you call the Bible or the New Testament. Was it not written and prophesied in the book of Jeremiah that the new covenant that God was to make with the house of Israel was that he would put his laws in their inward parts and write it in their hearts. That is the New Testament, not the book you call the New Testament which is of the letter. If men looked at what God has written on their hearts, then there would be no mistake or confusion. But the words of men are subject to private interpretation even when written by inspiration. After I left, my disciples were still on a journey of learning each day according to that which the Father gave to them. There were yet many things for them to learn but they were not yet ready to bear them while I was with them. In the New Testament church each man would know God for himself, just as I did. He would not have to ask another for that which is already his. If one continues to receive this fresh bread daily from the Father, he will continue to be transformed into the image of Christ even as I was."

I interrupted, "How can that be? So many people depend on the New Testament Bible for their knowledge of God."

"Even the letters in that book testify of what I just told you. Doesn't it say that in Christ is all knowledge and wisdom? Doesn't it say that the anointing which you have received of God abides in you and that you need not that another should teach you? Doesn't it say that the anointing is truth and shall teach you all things? Have you become so dependent on the words on paper that you no longer can see what has been written on your heart?"

There must have been something important that I had missed. This made little sense to me. "I was always taught that the New Testament was God's book to us. I was taught it was the way he spoke to us," I responded.

"No, that is not so. My purpose was to show my people the Jews first and those who were not my people that our Father had provided a new and better way. Not a way as was the Old Testament in parchment of paper but a new and living way where God would be our Father and we his sons and daughters. Does a Father communicate with his children through a book or does he prefer to deal with them directly? I came as a tree of life to restore that, which was lost in the Garden. I gave my life showing and telling about the kingdom of God that is within you that you might come boldly directly to our Father's throne without any partitions. As a Christian, why have you chosen to make my life and death of no effect by walking in the flesh instead of the spirit? Why have you put more trust in the teachings of others? Why have you decided that the book is a gift from God? In truth, by their teachings, churches have made the book more important than seeking knowledge and wisdom directly from the Father. And for the hardness of your hearts, the Father has made it a stumbling block to you. Can you remember the day when you were born again?"

"Yes," I answered.

"Tell me. When you felt the presence of our Father and invited him into your heart, did he reveal himself to you or speak to you directly or through a book?"

"Directly," I answered. "He spoke to my spirit directly."

"Yes", he answered. "And that was the foundation

of the church. Flesh and blood did not reveal that to you. You didn't believe because you read it in a book. You believed because you experienced or perceived the Father for yourself. You received his words directly. You need the words of the Father to overcome this world. When I told my disciples that if they continued in my words, they would know the truth and the truth would set them free. I was speaking the words of the Father and wanted them to continue to receive them from Him as I did. I made my words that which He spoke to me. One must remember that there was no written book of the New Testament at that time so they knew I was not talking about words in a book. I had told them many times that the words were not my own words and they could be one with the Father even as I was."

"How do I overcome this world? And why is that so important?" I asked.

Jesus answered. "This world that you see is a temporary place. From science you determine it to have a beginning and an end. From your own records of life you can see even your own life is as the grass of the field, as a vapor that appears for a while and vanishes away. You all place extreme importance in this world as if this is eternal. You become attached to the things you can have. For some it is people and for others possessions and still others seek power. Many seek all three. You spend much thought on what you will eat or drink or wear. You make decisions based on these attachments without regard that these things will pass away. Now inside you know the truth that these things are all to pass with time. Yet you continue to hold on to those things that you see, hear, touch, or smell. They become so real by your attachment that you shut out yourselves from seeking or knowing the truth of your real nature. You convince yourselves that only the things of these senses can be known. Why then will you look any further? These are the cares of this world. It is these things that you must overcome so you can see with that part of you that is not temporary. As long as temporal things monopolize your thoughts, they will control you and you will live a life that continues to perish with each passing day. Only when you overcome these things can you see clearly and awake to your true being as life eternal in God."

Jesus continued. "You have by choice trapped yourselves in these thoughts and they hold your attention. You walk around as men intoxicated with the cares of this world and therefore your vision is clouded. To be free, you must overcome these things by filling your thoughts with the knowledge of the truth. This knowledge is from the Father. Your receiving or hearing his words is your faith. This faith doesn't just believe words written in a book but rather sees the real substance of things. It is this faith as it is called that allows you to break free or overcome those things that you have allowed to hold you in bondage. This faith is seeing truth by hearing directly from God and not from flesh and blood."

"Why is that not the message we hear today in the churches? Why didn't the people of your times hear this message and record it?" I asked.

"But they did," he responded. "Have you not read in your book that I went about all the land preaching the glad tidings of the kingdom of God? Does it not say that I told them that the kingdom of God was not of this world nor in meat and drink? Did I not say when it was demanded of me when the kingdom shall come that I said the kingdom of God comes not with outward show but rather that the kingdom of God was within you? Did I not say that the kingdom of God was here now and the time was at hand? Did I not say to take no thought for what ye shall eat or wear and such? Did I not say that hearing from the Father was the foundation of my church? Did I not say the works I did you could do also? Did I not say I did what I heard spoken by the Father? Did I not say and was it not recorded that I said you all may be one with the Father even as I was one?"

He continued. "Indeed, these things were recorded. Those who were dull of hearing back then are no different then those who are now. Men still look for God in books and with the senses of this world.

They try and make that which is spiritual and eternal unto that which is physical and to perish with the using."

"But if the truth was so simple, why have we missed it? I asked.

"You have allowed a personal relationship to turn into a church organization much as the Jews of my time did. You say you are following God because your leaders use my name but they feed you their own bread. Instead of receiving your daily bread from heaven as I taught, some even call these men father and allow themselves to be spoon-fed from earth by the teachings of men. You worry about receiving a mark in your hand or forehead from the beast yet you ask not for the spiritual wisdom to understand what it is. And in failing to do so, you receive the mark in your mind or instead you fellowship with the beast choosing to take it in your right hand. You think that one day this mark will be needed to buy and sell food. And it is even now. But the real food is not that which perishes. Rather than take the free "manna" or bread that our Father offers us daily you choose to receive the spiritual mark or badge of servitude that comes from being fed by man's theology and dogma. This is the mark of the beast and it is today prevalent in your churches. It is in your organized churches where the seat of the antichrist is being established so that this spirit I speak of is sitting in the temple of God, as if it is God. The temple I am speaking about is not made with the hands of men."

As if anticipating my questions, Jesus continued. "Many are zealous but without knowledge. They seek the knowledge of books. They verse themselves in history and words and languages. They pride themselves in their understandings of biblical things and customs and details yet overlook the simplicity in Christ. They consider not that Christ was neither my last name nor the name of a man or one person. Christ was a title and is a divine expression of the Father. It is the hope of glory for all. They worship me as God when I told them not to even call any man good but our Father, which is in heaven. They form doctrines and rituals to honor me as God when I told them I could do nothing without the Father. They make statues of saints and pictures and images of me that bear likeness of their imaginations believing they are honoring God. They do this, even after they were instructed to have no graven images before the people. These images were neither to be of heaven or of earth. Have you not perverted and twisted the truth and made it of no effect?"

Suddenly I could say nothing. I was cut to the quick. Here I was thinking that I was a good Christian subjecting myself to my spiritual leaders and learning all about biblical history and things. After all, that's why I was here in the Holy Land I thought. When I was young I was raised a Catholic and knelt and prayed before statues and images but not in the last thirty years. And so what if I wore an image of a man on a cross on my neck or had pictures of Jesus for Bible markers. I didn't mean any harm by it. But now, I could see that these pictures and images did nothing to focus me on the Father. They only served to limit my comprehension of God. I thought to myself, God is not a man that he should be honored as such. How could a man, a picture or image reflex an accurate understanding of God?

There was a time when I had a direct experience of God's presence. Somehow I guess that I let others talk me out of it. I was soon back to the rituals of attendance and listening to preachers. I had said the Lords prayer often but when I came to the words "give us this day our daily bread," somehow I envisioned it as food for the flesh rather than the spirit. Because my pastor had so many years of schooling, I remember deciding that I would accept whatever he said. I never again thought of asking God for myself or even expecting God to talk to me directly. If all this were true that I was hearing from this man then I had truly detoured off the right path. Could all this be? I thought. Somehow I knew that what I was being told was true but my mind found it hard to let go of old teachings.

Finally, I spoke out. "Jesus, Somehow I know that what you are telling me is true but it is so hard to give up that which I have."

After a short pause, he continued. "That is because the light of God's anointing is in all men that come into this world. That part of you knows and can acknowledge truth. The teachings and stories of men over the years have provided a veil that has suppressed Truth. One cannot know the Father by the flesh. God is a spirit and only by his spirit, which he put in us, can we know him directly. If you deny its presence then how will you find it? I told my disciples that unless they were born again they could not see the kingdom of God. One has to die to the flesh to be born again to the spirit. I wasn't talking about physical death. The kingdom of God is here on earth now but it is a spiritual kingdom. It is the place one must operate to understand all things. If you receive my words now and do not allow them to be taken away by the cares or circumstances of this world or the teachings of men, then you will continue to know that which is true. In fact you will need me here no more. I told my disciples that I was going away. Yet I did not leave them alone. Now that they had believed they could ask the Father directly and he would answer them."

And upon his saying that, I saw the man who called himself Jesus no more. I somehow knew I would not be seeing him again. I must admit that a part of me wanted him back. It was so easy to become dependent on another to get answers. It was even easier than reading books. But the one thing for sure. I knew what it was like to know truth and that it was with me. He was right. What more need did I have of him. He finished his work a long time ago. Now it was my turn.

I sat motionless for some time. How long I do not remember. After seeing light again entering through the slits in the roof, I decided it was time to leave and find my way back to the group by whatever means possible. Somehow there was a new peace about me. I wasn't really worried about my predicament. After all, God was with me and I knew it. I knew I was going to get safely back and I held on to that truth and made a conscious effort to entertain no thoughts to the contrary. After carefully exiting the rock formation to avoid skinning myself, I turned about toward the road. Amazed at what I saw, I remained inwardly calm as I recalled my new experience. I slowly and deliberately made my way to the road. What my eyes beheld I refused to reason within myself. Nothing made sense to the flesh but I sensed I was a new creation where no explanation was necessary. There was only an inward knowing that said that all would be fine.

Chapter 6
Rescued at Last

As I approached the bus, people were beginning to re-board. I took special note that this was indeed the same people from my church group and the driver hurrying everyone aboard was the same as the day before. I quietly boarded without a word. I took a seat next to Judy without thinking and asked how long she thought we had been here.

"Been about three hours, I think," she answered and continued. " Where have you been? I looked for you after I got off the bus to sit in the shade but I supposed you stayed onboard." She looked for me? I asked myself shocked. I never knew she thought that I existed.

"Well, actually I got off the bus before the rest of the people and was sitting over there in the shade of the boulders on our left," I said as I looked her straight in the eyes. I wanted to say more but before I could she responded. "What boulders are you referring to?" To which I answered, "Those over there." And as I looked out to our left as the bus driver shifted into first gear and we started to roll, I saw nothing but desert.

"Never mind, I must have seen a mirage" I said now wondering what was happening to me. There were no boulders to be seen. I looked at my watch and saw it was still Tuesday as it was when we stopped. Could this all be a dream? Did I really even get off the bus? Yes, I must have because I got back on to sit with her just five minutes ago, I answered myself. Where have I been? I looked at my shoes and there was sand between the laces so I must have been somewhere in the desert. What really happened out there I don't know. But here I am now.

I sat quietly beside her without any more words exchanged. I thought through my whole experience. Was it a dream or not? I could not tell. Perhaps, I fainted in the desert. Yet I was neither thirsty nor hungry and I looked at my arms and they showed no signs of sunburn. This was too strange. It was the kind of thing that if you kept thinking about it, you might go crazy. I wrote it off as if saying, "I don't know." Here I was sitting by the girl I dreamed about and it really didn't matter. My priorities had changed. No longer was I focused on others. I sat motionless for the next hour refusing to consider my dilemma until we reached Cairo and our five-star hotel.

Chapter 7
At the Hotel in Cairo

It was there in the solitude of my room that this experience was replayed again and again in my mind. It didn't matter whether it was a dream, a vision or real. I was a changed person. I knew I had connected with the truth. The words, "you can ask the Father directly," rang over and over in my mind. I decided I would tell no one of my experience. It was a private thing and I was sure that most people wouldn't understand.

Yes, my eyes were opened. I knew I was connected to the Father. No one told me I just knew it. He would provide me with the answers to my questions. No longer did I need the man Jesus anymore. He had done his work and pointed the way. In my thoughts I said Father, people say there is only one way to God and that is Jesus. Yet what about all the rest of the religions in this world. Many of them also think they are the only way. Expecting an answer, my thoughts took form as if I already knew the answer and said to me.

"Yes, there is only one way to me."

To which my thoughts responded. "What religion is it?"

"It is not a religion my son. It is my spirit. No one can know me except by my spirit."

You mean that when Jesus said I am the way, the truth, and the life, no man comes to the Father but by me that he was not talking of himself or Christianity as a religion?

"Throughout time many men have searched and found my spirit. It has never been far away. Jesus was sent as a king and priest for his people to point them the way to me. Christ was a title given by his people. It meant my anointing spirit, a divine expression of myself. It is my spirit living in my creation. When he spoke he spoke not of himself but of me. He was saying that he existed by the way or path that is the true life to me. He existed not just on fleshly bread but on the bread of life, which is the spirit of life or truth that comes from me. That is the true life. It is a direct connection with me. That is the only way to me that all who will find me must come. It is not a religion or a method. It is not a theology or an organization. The way or path is a connection through my spirit to me. The link exists

to all my creation."

"There have been many messengers that I have sent. They have testified of these things. They have shown the way to men. And those who are ready; do listen and find. Those who do not listen; make up a religion of their own. Yet my spirit continues to draw all men. When they are ready; they will come."

After this, I drifted off to sleep and awoke refreshed in the morning. No longer was I interested in seeing the sights before our trip back to the states. I wanted to be alone and commune with the Father. There was yet much to learn. Skipping the tours, I remained in my room pondering what all this fuss was about in Jerusalem. After all, I was shown that God is not confined to a city such as Jerusalem but was with people everywhere. Basically the trip was commercialized and I got the impression the locals thought we were a bunch of sucker tourists that loved to buy trinkets, holy water and other mementos. Most of them were still waiting on a messiah and believed we were a foolish people.

This day I again excused myself from the tours and skipped lunch. While laying across the bed that was made while I was out to breakfast I asked the question I always wanted to ask. Why doesn't God just make a supernatural sign and speak to all the people from the heavens at one time so they get truth? And then from the depths of my spirit came the answer.

"I have nothing to prove to man. He is part of my creation. To him is given access to me at all times. A better question would have been, "How did my children get to the state of separation they are now in?" I have never deserted them that I should interrupt their choice in life and give them a sign and speak to them from the heavens. On earth your father provided for you in childhood and was there for counsel even while you were grown. Yet how many times did you seek him for counsel or understanding? Why is this?"

If I remember correctly, when I was of age my desire was mostly to make my own life. I wanted to chose my own friends and learn things for myself. I wanted to experience life based on choices that I alone made. I knew my father was available while he was here all along but I wanted to impress him by showing him I could make a success of myself on my own.

"Yes, in the things of the flesh it was so, and in the things of the spirit it was as the same thing. But since I already have knowledge of all things and your access is free, why do you rather refuse it to only discover it again? Shall I be impressed if you

discover that which already is known as if by some ability of your own you have done this, seeing that all things are of me? Along time ago, you decided to take that path and left that which was already yours only to in the end discover it again. I have not hidden my face from you. But you have turned your face from mine and in the experience lost your way. Your experience has clouded your sight in that the creature, which is made, cannot see that which from all is made. Yet it is present with you always. In the dispensation of the fulness of times all will be come together in me. In the meantime the circle plays itself out."

I responded speaking loudly as if I needed to say what was on my mind. "I do not remember this time you speak of where I turned away and became lost. But in this circle you speak of, people are hurt! Men are killed! Injustices take place and sorrow is great. Poverty exists and pain and suffering is present everywhere."

"To him that is intoxicated with the life in the flesh, all these things you speak of do exist. Consider the animals. Each one has a predator. Each one has its time of hunger and time of filling and even a time of death. Do they complain or curse me? Are they not acquainted with poverty and sorrow? Yet how do they see it? Are you not living in a creature I have created that is also to return to the dust? Shall it not

also experience these things as I have foreordained? As long as you attach yourself to the creature that you call man you are in bondage to that creature. You experience these things but where are they? Where is your suffering? Where then are your pain and sorrow and poverty and death? These things have moved you only because you have lost sight of that which you are. These things are a most natural part of the creature but to you all illusions. These things you make as though they are a permanent part of you yet you can see they pass as a twinkling moment of what is called time. What then is pain and suffering except that which you have created for yourselves?"

Though there was no roughness in the answer, for fear I dared not to ask more. There was too great a response to my question and the answer was more than my mind could bear. I went out on the verandah outside of the double doors to my window and gazed at the great city of Jerusalem. "Oh Jerusalem! Jerusalem! You that kill the prophets!" I spoke as it rang throughout my thoughts. I continued gazing in amazement of the colorful city I saw.

It was time to head back home the next day. But first Pastor Jenkins would grace us with a sermon in a small room the hotel had reserved just for such purposes. I cleaned up and joined with the others to wait there for our "Sermon in the Holy Land". Right on time, Pastor Jenkins went to the podium and asked a couple of parishioners to lead us in "Amazing Grace" and "When We All Get to Heaven".

As I listened rather than sing to the second song, I thought it was rather foolish. We were singing about a day of rejoicing when we get to heaven and resigning ourselves to this woeful life here now. As if we couldn't rejoice in the present, I thought. The line "when we all see Jesus we'll sing and shout the victory" especially grieved my spirit now as I thought of what I had learned. This journey and hope on earth wasn't about getting to Heaven and seeing Jesus. It was about finding God's divine expression in us. It was about Christ; the anointing of God; his spirit in us; our hope of his presence here now. It was not about seeing Jesus. After all, I had seen him and that is not the message he had for me. It was not even the message of the book we called the Bible. In it, the hope it talked about was to find Christ in us, our hope of glory. The writers left off the word Jesus and used the title only. Now I understood why.

The sermon today, after opening prayer by brother Ledford, was on the Holy City of Jerusalem and its importance to us Americans. As pastor Jenkins read Old Testament scriptures about the city of Jerusalem, he expounded on the scriptures and their significance as his theology books had taught him. I could not help to wonder why it was that he would spend most of his time telling us about what the book said rather than what God had said or showed him.

My mind recalled that most all the sermons I had ever heard were this way. It was "the Bible says". Yet I remember reading in that same book that if a man speak, let him speak as the oracle or mouth-piece of God. Whatever happened to that verse I thought. And Jesus told me he even told his disciples that they were to speak what they heard in their ear even as he did. He was talking about our spiritual ear of course but regardless there seemed to be very little life in the words of this pastor. He talked about Jerusalem being the Holy City of God. He talked about the importance of our protecting the Jews. He talked about the city of Jerusalem's future place in prophecy.

I then asked God, not even thinking about where I was at this moment. "What made this city so holy or sacred?" As the voice of the pastor faded to the background, my thoughts as if they had life of their own spoke.

"I do not live in buildings made with man's hand. Neither do I require a city built with man's material and sweat. Am I flesh and blood that I should delight in these things? Are my people limited to

one race or origin? Am I not creator of all men? For who and what is a Jew? Do I delight on the outward or inward man?"

I knew I did not have to answer these questions. I knew the answers and I needed not to ask this foolish question again. Why is it that we accept these things the pastor was preaching without question? I thought. We sit and nod our head in agreement and challenge nothing. No wonder the church requires us as a confession of faith to acknowledge the Bible as it exists as the Word of God. Our acceptance of it keeps us from thinking or asking God for ourselves. And since we give so much credence to education of the pastor we assume that he knows the answers or what the book means better than we could ourselves. My confidence in what had been taught in the past was quickly fading and at that moment I made up my mind to consult God before establishing the thing pastors called knowledge.

The sermon gradually changed into an altar call. This was the time allotted for an individual to invite Jesus into his heart and make a confession of faith. I now believed it would be more accurate if they said a confession of belief rather than faith.This is because the pastor was saying all we had to do was to believe Jesus was God who took on flesh and died for our sins and if we believed we would go to heaven when we died. And of course "This is true" he would say and also "because the Bible tells us so." Yet even with my mind I had to question this. How does believing make something true? I believed that Santa Claus was real for better than 10 years and even my parents told me so. Even that did not make it true.

Faith had to be more than just believing or it was of no effect. One can believe a lie with all one's heart and that doesn't make it true. I now knew that faith had to be more. Faith needed to be a seeing of Truth. It had to be seeing that which things are made of. It was either there or it wasn't. It had to be more than believing.

What a joke, I thought. All my life I have been building a case with blocks that were part of somebody else's foundation. I have been establishing beliefs based on the hearsay and reading of men. Now I could see how important it was for every man to seek God for himself. Otherwise he would subject himself as a sheep to the foxes in sheep's clothing. "No more for me", I said out loud forgetting where I was. Fortunately only a few had heard me and from them I received a quick disturbing look.

No one answered the altar call. But that was not unusual. Most of the people here had been going to church for over 20 years. Being away from church for so long, I was pretty well the junior among them. The service was soon over and people were shaking hands and congratulating the pastor on his great sermon.

As he caught me on the way out he asked, “Joe, have you been enjoying yourself on this trip? Have you been sick? We missed you on several tours.”

It was kind of him to notice, I thought before I said. “Pastor Jenkins, I have never been better and my life will never be the same again”. To which he smiled and commented on what a holy place this was and something about how it had that effect on everyone that visits here. I nodded knowing that he really didn’t understand what I was saying and I returned to my room to pack for the trip back tomorrow.

Chapter 8
Getting Ready for the Return

Back in my room, I was alone again. As I arranged my suitcase, I was looking forward to getting home but I must admit there was a fear inside me that whatever had happened would go away when I returned. Still, I knew from what I was learning that location had little to do with my experience. What is the matter with us people, I thought. We have places that we attribute some holiness to. After all, each week the pastor would say before his sermon "Welcome to the house of the Lord." How could the church building be God's house? If God is omnipresent, as I had been taught, then why would we call one place his house and not another? Were we all so caught up in repeating phrases that we actually believed it?

In childhood, my brother and I were raised Catholics. We had Holy water yet we never understood what made it more holy than the water we drank. We were taught the 10 commandments and it said not to have any graven images before us neither of heaven nor of earth. Yet our church was filled with statues and images of apostles, saints and even Jesus. My brother who was a year older than I didn't seem to understand it. He had so many questions and the answers from our catechism just didn't seem to answer them. Shortly after confirmation, he decided to not go anymore and my parents didn't resist. Myself, I didn't know what to make of it. Believing what I was told seemed okay to me even if I didn't understand. Anyway, I decided that if he didn't have to go then neither should I go. That was the end of that saga in my life.

But now my eyes were opening and it was plain to see that most people are like sheep. They will follow a spiritual leader without questioning things. Perhaps, we felt it was too much work to think for ourselves? Perhaps, we give too much credit to those placed over us? Perhaps, we don't really believe but just feel accepted by following the crowd? Yes, maybe we are all blind following each other but really don't know why.

"Father", I said out loud. "Why are we so blind to what seems like simple things to reason for ourselves?" As I yielded my thoughts they were replaced.

"My children find that which they earnestly seek for. If one seeks for agreement with others more

than a desire for truth, then the desire to please other men and be accepted will blind him to the simple truth before him. One cannot serve opposing desires. One will win out and draw no attention to the other. That is why though I am always present, I am not yet found by many. A man's life comes out of the abundance of his heart. If his treasure in his heart is in the temporal things of this world, then that is all he will see. But if instead he chooses truth above all things, even life as he knows it himself, I will be found of him. And in me is all truth and life. We will supper together and the bread he receives from me shall sustain him."

Suddenly it seemed so simple. I was eating this bread that was spoken of. It was the true bread that Jesus spoke about that comes from heaven. Surely, what he called heaven could not be far away nor a physical place. The word heaven must have meant the spirit since God is a spirit and that is where he resides. And that location is everywhere. The bread must be God's words. It is given freely but only if you look with all your heart. And oh how my heart burned within for more, I thought.

"Though many children seek the praise of their father on earth, they seek the praise of men above that of their Father, which is in heaven. And in the earth, they have their reward of men yet before their very eyes it is destroyed as if by fire. But he who

seeks my praise above men is rewarded on earth and in the life to come."

"What is it my Father that pleases you that we should receive your praise?"

"Though I am not a man, my pleasure could be compared to the image of a father in the flesh. Does he who on earth and made in my image have pleasure with his children? Is he a father to them and they children to him? Do they not delight in his presence and seek his counsel? Is he not pleased in all of this? He that is born of me has also a spirit that is connected to me whose life is eternal. I give life to the flesh yet I delight not in flesh but in him that is a son to me. It is this communion that I myself delight in. If you delight yourself in me, then are we one and there is nothing that I will withhold of all that you ask. For the entire world and its fullness is mine."

"Why do we not choose what you describe to me? Why do we create religions about you when we can have a relationship with you?"

"I created man's spirit with a free will to make choices. As part of my creation he has always had a connection to me. It is self evident that man would not exist if I did not exist. His existence itself testifies to this. In me he lives and breathes and has

his being. Much like an earthly son leaves his father to become one for himself, so has the spirit that I have given man chosen to leave me and make a god of himself and in doing so forgotten me. He has become so attached to that of his own makings that he has lost sight of me in his intoxication with the life he has chosen."

"But then how is there hope for him?"

"From time to time I have sent those who commune and have knowledge of these things to be a beacon to other men. They speak my words. Those who will hear them and understand break free and those who will not, for now, do not. Nevertheless, men persecute those whom I send, because of many who rebel and will not come to me. But this will not be forever, for all that is flesh is temporal. For all men who go the path of separation or darkness as men call it are doomed to failure. Without me, there can be no life and so to attach oneself to that which dies is death. It will never have life of its own. And so in the fullness of times all will cry out and come full circle and return to me."

"But we were taught that there is no hope for those who reject you and they will burn in hell forever!"

"Do those who come to me; come to me because of their goodness? Do those who come to me; come to

me because they have earned it? Do those who come to me; come to me because they are smarter than the rest? Do I favor one child over another? No, I say. My spirit shall draw all men to me but each man in his own order. Time is not a constraint to me. For the spirit in men, when they finally see the fruitlessness of their path, they turn to me and find me when they seek me with all their heart. So to him that is not yet ready let him remain so for now because every man's harvest shall come. I have ordained it since the foundation of the world. This I will accomplish in the dispensation of the fullness of times."

With this, I finished packing and fell soundly off to sleep. When I woke up, my alarm had 5 minutes left before it would go off. I reset it and went about my daily routine of getting ready for breakfast. I checked my baggage downstairs with the groups so it would be processed automatically at the airport. I kept a small flight bag with my incidentals to carry on and use during the long flight back.

Breakfast was a noisy blur. Everyone was talking at what seemed like the same time about what wonderful buys they had made. They talked about how beautiful the sites were that we had visited. They talked about the accommodations and the food. They talked about coming back to this holy place. They talked about their many travels, their fine jewelry and their wonderful pastor. No one seemed to listen. They just all talked.

Conversations with people no longer interested me. They suddenly all seemed so shallow. Like the time I had recorded the telephone conversation of a friend and myself for 60 minutes. Afterwards, I couldn't remember what we really talked about so I played it back. In the conversation we accomplished nothing except to lift ourselves up as if we had all the solutions to the world's problems. Our 60 minutes were spent criticizing governments, politicians, sports teams and people in general like we knew how to do a better job and what was best for everyone else. And when we were done talking I remember feeling like we were better for our conversation. Such foolishness I now thought. Are we all drunks as surely these people here right now seem to me?

Chapter 9
The Trip Home

We were shuttled to the airport in Jordan. Then a two-legged trip to New York remained. I wasn't exactly excited about passing through London and then through New York again. A quick stop in London would be okay, but the customs in New York and having to switch planes again for a hop into Cincinnati was nothing to look forward to. It was December 21st and we were to pick up Pan Am Flight 103 in London to New York. The plane was a 747 and would certainly be packed with people trying to get home before Christmas.

Amid the noise at the airport I sat with our group in the gate area. My ticket and passport was in my hand. But my interest was not to the people around me but to the discovery I had made inwardly of my Father. I must admit that even though I knew better and it was so foolish, there was a small fear that God would not follow me home. "Father," I said to myself, "Leave me not as I leave this land and guide me closer to you." The distractions around me were too great to focus on my thoughts. But as surely as I had asked, a sense of urgency not to leave arose from my very being. I became anxious and wanted a clearer response but my emotions prevented me from receiving more. I could find no peace among the noise and commotion of the airport.

As I heard the call for our flight, my anxiety level rose. All I knew is that all that had happened to me on this trip I had accepted as real. I made a quick decision that live, die, sink or swim, I would be obedient to my new relationship. I pushed myself close to Pastor Jenkins and with some noticeable nervousness said. "Pastor Jenkins, I've decided to stay over another day or two. I know it is unusual and I signed an understanding of responsibility before we came here but I need to stay here for now. I have my charge card and will make my own necessary airline changes."

"Is everything okay Joe? You have been acting rather strange and keeping to yourself the last portion of this trip. Your luggage is already loaded and I have never before had a request like this. You are putting me in an awkward position", he said inquisitively.

I didn't give him an answer. What could I say? I just looked at him with my mind already made up. "Call the church or me at home the minute you get home.

You should have told me sooner," he scolded as if he were my father. Then he moved on to see the rest were boarding okay. Others turned and gave me a strange look wondering why I was separating myself from the group. Even I didn't know at the time so I immediately headed for transportation back to the town to get alone with whatever this was that was keeping me here.

On the way back, doubts and fears crept into my mind. What was I doing? This was crazy behavior. Now I have gone and done it. I've gone off the deep end. These thoughts and more bombarded my mind as if to tear me apart. A battle was going on in my mind as if a part of me were dying and trying to hold on. "No," I said out loud, as the cab driver gave me a strange look. Then I returned to my thoughts saying to myself "Let the old part of me die that I might live in newness of spirit wherever it takes me." Peace then came over me and I remember no thought but the next thing I heard was the cab door opening in front of the hotel. I paid and went inside with only my small bag of incidentals I had packed for the long trip back.

In my room, I laid across the bed without thought, knowing I was right where I was supposed to be. I refused to think about when or if I would even leave this place. I was at peace and that is all that mattered. Without eating, I fell asleep and slept soundly for 18 hours straight, waking up at 6:00 Jordan time. I knew I would be checking out. I don't remember having a conversation with my Father but it was as if I had. I heard no words, I just knew. God was with me and no one had to tell me. I could not differentiate between his thoughts and mine so I just flowed with things. I showered and checked out of the hotel. There was a stir around me. The foreigners I could not understand but the Americans that were headed for the shuttle to the airport were buzzing with the news. Flight Pan AM 103 had crashed yesterday above Scotland. All 259 including passengers and crew were dead. Even some that were on the ground were killed. I would not be calling Pastor Jenkins when I got home.

I thought tears should be rolling from my eyes. After all I knew many of these people. And oh yes, Judy was on that flight too. But there were no tears and no sorrow for them or her. I had an inward knowing that all things were in their place and this was dominant in my thoughts. My emotion was no different than when a deer was shot or a cat or dog lay in the road. I thought, how insensitive I am, but I quickly gave those thoughts up for a New World that I had discovered. I gave them up for a city where there was no pain, no tears and no sorrow; a city without thirst or hunger; a city without struggle, without violence and without lies. And this city was inside of me.

I contacted the airlines and made new arrangements with my credit card. That afternoon, I was on my way back to Cincinnati but I was no longer the same. I was a new creature. Old things had passed away and all things were as if new. They could call me crazy but I wouldn't trade it for all the gold in the world.

Chapter 10
Home Again and The Story

I arrived home in Cincinnati in time for Christmas. But it was a sad time for many of the locals here. There was much mourning. Talk shows and newspapers were talking about the crash. There were eulogies and swelling words for those from our city. There were flowers and color guards. There was pomp and there was ceremony. Still, I never came forward to say that I was supposed to be on that flight. The need to do so was not in me. The church got a new pastor and nobody seemed to notice that I no longer attended. I knew that I had not really escaped death just because I was still here. I liked it that way. I felt like a new man. The old man had died with those on the plane yet I lived. I was awake to the spirit within me and it was more real than the old life I had known.

I found a new church and continued my relationship with the Father. Soon, I was made unwelcome in this church. I couldn't share the things that I had received. This church told me that God doesn't talk with men anymore. They said HE did in the old days but now we had a Bible and that is sufficient till we die and get to heaven.

Thinking it would be good if I had a heart to heart talk with the pastor, I asked Pastor Mosley if he would stay over after service to counsel me concerning the problem I was having at his church. He indicated he would be delighted and always looked forward to helping to steer men to the right path. I was told to wait in his office. It reminded me of Pastor Jenkins office back in the beginning. Pastor Mosley was a generous man who it seemed was always helping the poor or giving his time getting involved with right to life and other church related organizations. He was not a shy speaker and always seemed to smile. “What was I going to say?” I thought out loud. And then it came to me that I should say very little but rather ask questions to gain a clearer understanding of what belief system existed at this church that I had found so common in others.

Soon the pastor walked in. He sat in the chair behind his desk and asked, “Joe, exactly what is the problem that you are having that I can help you with?”

To which I responded, “Pastor Mosley, I would like to gain a clearer understanding of what you see as God’s message and plan for us in simple terms without just quoting Bible scriptures.” I then remained silent and ready to soak up every word.

With eagerness, he responded, "I'm so glad you came to talk with me one on one. Sometimes we do get wrapped up in the Word of God and forget to put it in more simplistic terms. I noticed you were having a problem ever since you came to us. In this I would be most happy to counsel you."

He continued. "Let me start it simply by saying that God wants to be our master. He wants us to enter into a love relationship with him. A relationship very similar to marriage partners and that is why I always say that as Christians we are married to Christ. We have all been born into the curse of Adam. We are lost and need a sacrifice to save us from eternal damnation. The good news is that man can be saved from this eternal damnation by repentance and his believing in God's coming to this earth and sacrificing himself on the cross for our sins. And our sin is the nature of the beast that is in all men, which is the curse of Adam. This sacrifice, if we choose to believe it, gains us the forgiveness of our sins. It is a gift to all but can be received only by believing that God so loved the world that he himself took on flesh and sacrificed himself for the remission of our sins. It annuls the nature of the beast we were born with."

As he took a breath, I quickly asked, " Is this Jesus, who came in the flesh and is recorded as dying on the cross the eternal God himself?"

"Yes", he responded without hesitation and continued. " If we reject this message then we reject God. As a result if we do not accept this message prior to death, our soul, which lives forever will go to hell to live with the devil in misery, suffering and separated from God forever and ever with no hope of ever reconnecting with God."

"Doesn't God love us with an everlasting love? Doesn't his mercy endure forever?" I asked.

"Of course," he responded, as if surprised by my question. "But God is also a wrathful God. If his plan for us is rejected during this lifetime then you will be separated from that love forever. That is why it is so important for everyone to preach this message so that by believing it many of the hearers may accept this sacrificial offering for the remission of their sins and be saved from eternal punishment. God loves everyone and wants everyone to be saved."

"Doesn't that make God's love conditional?" I asked.

"No"! He answered with authority. "Everyone has a free will to accept his plan. His love is unconditional to all. He died for all, but you have to believe this by faith to accept it. By your response you determine the outcome. It is not God's fault if you reject him. And after rejection, it is too late for his love."

"Is there anything else I must believe? Is believing that Jesus is God and that he came and died for my sins the only requirement to be saved from this misery and suffering after death that you speak of?"

"Well," he added. "Of course you must also repent and after you are saved and are introduced to the Bible, then you must recognize it as the written Word of God. If you reject his written Word for us then you reject God. I'm not saying you can't be saved without the Bible. We preach the message to people all over the world that can't even read or have never seen a Bible. Because they believe our words they are saved and come to God. However, after they are introduced to the Bible they must believe his written Word is without errors. Things like believing the Virgin Birth, the physical confession of your faith, the physical resurrection of Jesus and his deity are a requirement and clearly spelled out in the Bible to the Christian."

"Can't they still be saved and reject some of its writings?" I interjected quickly.

"No," he responded. "If they truly believed the message then they will recognize the written Word as HIS when they do get to read it or get someone to read it to them. You must have faith to be saved. Simply put, you must believe the message or be damned. That is not my opinion but rather what God says. He loves you and gave his life for you. It is for you to accept or reject the message. I am only a minister of HIS Word."

"Why is it that you say we are to have a marriage or love relationship with God yet instead of communicating directly as one would with a wife or mate we have to receive instructions from a book?" I asked politely.

"That is a good question," he answered. "There are many voices in this world and we must be sure we are not hearing the voice of Satan, the enemy. The book is given by God and is our road map to God and his truths. If what we hear from what we think is God doesn't line up with the Bible then we know it is not true; it is from the enemy; we must reject it. The Bible has existed longer than any other religious book in history and God has not allowed it to be destroyed through wars, famines and the dark ages. Its preservation through history itself speaks of the divine intervention of God and the Bible and its purpose in our lives."

I had heard enough and could see the bondage this

story held over its believers but interjected one last question before I thanked him for his time. "What of the people who go through life and never hear this message?"

He responded, hesitatingly, "It's possible that God may have a special dispensation for them. I don't know exactly. His Word does say that the Gospel will be preached to all creatures and if it is preached and rejected then all hope is lost."

I thanked him and though he asked me to pray with him, I excused myself and said I wanted to think over all that he had said this day.

He then responded. "My door is always open and I will be praying you make the right choice."

That was one prayer I was certain would be answered.

Chapter 11
Pondering The Story

Amazed is a word that was insufficient to describe my feelings as I pondered the Christian message and plan for mankind that I had heard this day which in my thoughts I refer to as The Story. Such power over people in a story is simply amazing, I thought. The Story was very familiar but no longer would I struggle with it. This last pastor had put it in such simple terms. The spirit of the Story was what held its captives prisoners. It masqueraded itself as the good news. I had heard that someone once said that religion was the opiate of the people and I didn't remember who but now I got a glimpse of what he was talking about.

I pieced the story again and again together in my mind. This was the same story I was fed all my life with small variations. I repeated it over and over and in my mind it went something like this. There was a God who loved us and created us in his image but because of one man's sin we were born into a curse. But this curse would not last forever because God so loved us that he would be born of a Virgin and take on this flesh himself and sacrifice his body and blood so we could receive the remission of our sins by his sacrifice and be free from the curse. Now, we all couldn't be there for this sacrifice but if we were told The Story and believed it and confessed it through the hearing from others then we could be saved from the curse and after death go to live with God in a place called Heaven. However, if we rejected The Story, our curse would remain and when we died God would judge us and send us to misery and suffering in a place called Hell where we would remain forever and ever.

Even though God loves us with an everlasting love and is merciful, we have this time period of this life to either accept or reject this love by accepting or rejecting The Story to receive the consequences described. This God has provided us with preachers and a book called the Bible that tells us all these things and therefore we are without excuse if we refuse to believe The Story. It is the only true story and any other story is a lie. Believing The Story is the only way to avoid this Hell of eternal misery and suffering and the only way to know God.

That was pretty well it in a nutshell, I thought. Of course, there are always small variations. But pretty well that was The Story. Looking at the whole story, it was obvious there were many things that made no sense. Like a fairy tale or fable such as Santa Clause it has benefits to offer the believer but it is still not founded on truth. Yet even the Santa Clause story is powerful enough to hold children's thoughts captive for many years until a peer or their parents or life reveal it to them.

First of all, The Story paints a picture of God as a Father who loves us with a love greater than our earthly fathers do but has us born into a curse because of one man's sin. Then it makes him a very impersonal Father who instead of speaking directly to us has us propagate The Story to others by a Book or men's repeating of The Story. Then it would have us believe God gives us the condition that the hearer must believe The Story in this lifetime or lose all chance of ever being with their heavenly Father again. It makes him a God who gives us free will to accept or reject The Story and based on that decision when we die be saved or condemned to misery and suffering with no hope of changing the outcome. It portrays a God of love that punishes the MAJORITY of his children with everlasting punishment based on believing The Story as the only true story over the multitude of stories that are in and believed by others in this world today. It portrays a God that loves us so much that he makes a decision to make himself sinful flesh so that he can sacrifice that flesh for the remission of our sins.

The people propagating The Story seemed nice enough. They would be considered by most as good and gentle people. But how could the story be true?

And I thought to myself. If I were a father here on earth with my limited capacity to love, could I do such as this thing to the children I love? I have seen fathers on this earth welcome back their sons and daughters even after they had been rejected and spit on by them for much of a lifetime. Does love have a time boundary to God, yet not to some here on earth that were created in his image with only a portion of that love?

No, I couldn't imagine how this would be so. I have tasted his love and I have heard his voice and he lives and breathes in the thoughts I think. There is no separation from him except in our consciousness for he has shown me he was with me always, even when I knew it not. No, again I thought, God is not man that his love has boundaries. He has enough for all of his creation. It will surface, no matter how long it takes yet it has been and is there always. God is present everywhere for he has created all things and neither height of a Heaven nor depth of a Hell can separate him from us. God is much bigger than we can paint him and limiting him to the flesh of one man or one son is truly a narrow understanding of truth.

I spoke with a number of believers at the church just as I had with Pastor Mosley. Most of the believers I had talked to that believed The Story had a common denominator. They believed that the Bible as it exists today is a divine and extremely accurate if not perfect or infallible record of God's people and his works, words, and instructions for us. They especially recognized the gospels and the rest of the New Testament as being without error.

Reading the books of the Bible in the light of the churches teachings continually reinforces The Story. One cannot question The Story validity if the book is considered as truth. Those who accept this as true without question have placed themselves under the Bible's power and dominion. There can be no alternatives or other truth because of the bondage of its words and their belief and unwillingness to consider other stories or question The Story. Therefore, I set myself to read the gospels of Matthew, Mark, Luke and John and the rest of the New Testament thoroughly over the next few weeks to see if there were inconsistencies that are not told to the people that would lead one to a different conclusion of accuracy. I took a two weeks vacation from work and spent 12 hours a day reading and cross-referencing its content.

At the end of the 2 weeks, I was surprised to find so many things that were not in agreement. There were a few that I could not even imagine what the explanation could be.

The first was the genealogy in the first Chapter of Matthew. It is an area that few people read for themselves because it contains so many "begats" that it is boring to most. I set out to count the generations from Abraham to Christ. It said there were fourteen generations from Abraham to David and fourteen generations from David to the carrying away into Babylon and fourteen generations from the carrying away into Babylon unto Christ. That makes 42 generations total. I counted every "begat" many times and could only find 41 generations to Jesus with one missing from the carrying away of Babylon unto Jesus who is called Christ. This at first caused a problem because I was always told the Jews took their genealogy very seriously. It was also a problem especially since this is suppose to be a divinely inspired and written record of God's people without errors. There were only 13 generations in the book from the carrying away of Babylon unto Jesus, who is called Christ but after reading the book of James I decided to dismiss it since I remembered reading that by his own free will Christ "begat" us who are in Christ which would mean that we Christians by adoption were of the Christ generation which though not mentioned in the Matthew "begats" could be used to explain the missing generation that made 42 to Christ. That would not be serious enough of a problem to me since an explanation was possible by inference or supposition. However, when I read Luke Chapter 3 versus 23 through 38 I found the genealogy again but this time starting at Jesus and going back to Abraham and before. The problem here was major as Luke indicated 56 instead of 42 generations from Abraham to Jesus. And if that wasn't enough, only 16 of the names in the lineage matched with Matthew. Now that is a problem, I thought.

This could seriously hamper one's belief that the Bible as it exists is an accurate book and deserving to be referred to as the word of God. And if one of the books in it contains erroneous information then doesn't that invalidate the pretext of its divine intervention for accuracy and translation from God. Do we put our faith in every word of the rest of it? Having one book everybody goes by may be convenient to keep people in line and in believing the same story. But is it true?

The second concerned Judas Iscariot who betrayed Jesus. In Matthew 27 versus 3 to 5 it indicated that Judas, which had betrayed him, when he saw that he was condemned, repented himself, and brought again the thirty pieces of silver to the chief priests and elders, saying he had sinned in that he had betrayed the innocent blood. It then said he cast down the pieces of silver in the temple, and departed, and went and hanged himself. Yet in Acts Chapter 1 verses 15 to 19 Peter stood up to speak about replacing Judas as an apostle and says that Judas purchased a field with his iniquity money he had received and falling headlong that he burst and all his bowels gushed out. That is a different method of death and story than was described in Matthew.

Then there is the conversion of Saul in Acts 9:7 and again in Acts 22:9 that conflicts in the question " Did the men with Saul hear a voice or not". Yes in the the first story and no in the second telling. And if that is not enough it is covered again in Acts 26:14 where one time he tells the story the men with him fell to the ground yet in Acts 9:7 they stood speechless. All this in the same book, by the same writer, telling the same story and contradicting itself.

There are many more such as Jesus' last words before he gave up the ghost differ in John 19 verse 30 where it is recorded his last words were "Father, into thy hands I commend my spirit;" from Luke 23 verse 46 where it is recorded his last words were "It is finished." The two other gospels give even a completely different phrase as his last words and record him as saying "My God, my God, why have you forsaken me?"

Romans Chapter 1 verse 3 says that Jesus Christ was born of the seed of David according to the flesh.

Now Joseph, who was Mary's husband, was of the seed of David according to the flesh as recorded in the Matthew genealogy. However, both Matthew and Luke say that Mary was a virgin and was not impregnated by Joseph, which if that were true would not make Jesus of the seed of David, by that lineage. Jesus would be of the seed or son of Mary but not of Joseph.

Perhaps, some will say Luke followed Mary's fathers lineage to prove the seed of David by the flesh but if so why would Matthew follow Joseph's lineage when it not applicable to a virgin birth? And if as in Luke 1 versus 5 and 36 Mary is related to Elizabeth then it would make her of the Aaronic line and not of the Davidic line as was prophesied. And to further complicate trying to make any excuses I found that 1 Chronicles 3 versus 11 and 12 had three generations of names in the lineage that were not in the one by either Matthew or Luke.

Again in the account of Mark Chapter 15 and Matthew Chapter 28, Jesus died the evening before the Sabbath and arose the morning after the Sabbath. He was not suppose to rise until he was in the belly of the earth for 3 days and 3 nights as was Jonah. It was spoken of a number of times and is propagated by the Christian churches and in a statement of faith by the Catholic denomination that after 3 days and 3 nights he arose from the dead. However, the record here indicates no more than 2 nights and 1 full day passed and he was risen.

I pondered all this and thought to myself. All of this and more we were fed without questioning and studying for ourselves. Yes, the Book contains truths and inspired writings but through the years we have accepted every word as true and our elders have asked us to believe it all by faith. But believing a lie will not make it true. If the entire book was divinely put together by God as the church claimed then it would seem to me it would not have such errors. A brief study of published Christian statements of faith reveals the Bible is to be the supreme standard by which all human conduct, creeds, and religious opinions should be tried.

It occurred to me to revisit Pastor Mosley who had been patient enough to put the story in such simple terms for me without using or quoting scripture. I was curious what his response might be to all my research. I wondered if it would cause him to rethink his position concerning the Bible as being a work without errors that God wanted us to use to filter what we hear from what might not be from God. I called for an appointment and he seemed happy to hear from me.

The next Sunday I again entered his office and explained what I had been doing the past couple of weeks. As I finished my discourse on the subject, his smile was gone and he opened his mouth.

"Joe" he said. "The Bible is a spiritual book. Much of it may not make sense to your logical mind but regardless it is true. It is all about faith. It all fits together. Many men have through the years tried to disprove it and failed. That is why it has survived for thousands of years." Getting noticeably louder he continued. "There are no errors in the Bible to one who has God's spirit."

I quickly interjected. "But how can it be that two stories can be so different and still be the same?"

Getting noticeably irritated as if I came to fight him, he answered. "People when telling a story see different things. It doesn't make it untrue. At an accident, one passerby notices the color of the cars while another sees the medical personnel while another just sees the victims. Each one will tell you what he saw differently but it is the same accident."

"Yes Pastor Mosley, I understand that but here we have not portions or pieces of the same accident but differences of opinions about the same piece that contradict each other. Are there 42 or 56 generations between Abraham ...?"

Before I could finish, he interrupted. "That is not

important! What is important is your soul. There is an explanation for all these things. In time we will find them but now by faith we know that the Bible is God's manual for us and it is true. God confounds the wise by their reasoning with the mind. Your logical mind is not the way to God."

I quickly ended the conversation by apologizing for taking up his valuable time and excused myself. His demeanor changed quickly back to a gentle man with a smile as if he just caught himself off guard going somewhere he did not want to go and turned back to that place that he was.

As I returned home and thought on these things, it seemed to me that we Christians have trapped ourselves again under a law. The Jews of the Old Testament times lived under the law of the Old Testament. Jesus had told me he came to fulfill the prophecies of the old law and show us a new and better living way. He never wrote a book nor was it even recorded in the Gospels that he commanded anyone to write a New Testament book. Yet here we were in New Testament times with another book we call the New Testament, which we have made an unquestionable law. We have been made to believe in its total accuracy of translation and content by a concept the church system refers to as faith. I looked up the word testament and found it to mean witness, testimony or evidence. Jesus had told me in my encounter on the road to Egypt that his testament was in his life. Though the book contains many truths and records concerning God it is only man's futile attempt to create another law, which again puts him in bondage. Bondage he cannot leave without accepting rejection by his own people much as Jesus did in his day.

Days passed and I shared my findings with other Pastors and Ministers but most accused me of having a devil. They believed The Story with such fervor that they would shut their ears and repeat scripture to me as if it was to have some magical effect. One however, did listen somewhat and came up with a plausible explanation to the genealogy as I had surmised in my study but when I interjected the genealogy in 1st Chronicles he could not explain it and dismissed the importance. From there it was the same explanation over and over again which, was that you have to accept the book by faith and not use your reasoning mind. In other words, they told me that there was just no way for me to understand the truth with certainty without first believing The Story. They said I was lost and needed Jesus in my life.

Nevertheless, I made up my mind to continue looking for a fellowship of believers where I could feel at home. There must be more Christians who know these things, I thought. And if they were out there, I would find them.

Chapter 12
Still Searching for a Church

Months passed and I was still searching for a body of like-minded believers. I found another church to attend. But that didn't last very long. All I did was share what was spoken to me and they said I had a devil. If I wanted to brood, I could. Instead I took the better choice and entered again into the gates of this city which they knew not of. This was the spiritual city that I had found which healed my wounds. It was the city where the voice of the Spirit of God flowed freely.

As the years passed, I talked about God and his plan to the people of the Christian churches. The things that His spirit had revealed to me most people shunned aside. It just didn't agree with their theology books and what they said the Bible said. To hear the Spirit of God now was to be crazy. I thought to myself that it was a good thing Jesus was not walking in his flesh today. The churches that worship him and use his name would expel him for claiming he heard the voice of his Father God. Yet even their book records Jesus saying “He that hath an ear, let him hear what the spirit says”. They would surely point him to the Bible and say that this was God’s word for us now.

Part of me was really disappointed but before it could take hold I would remember to walk in again to the place where discouragement didn’t exist. God had showed me his kingdom and I could go in and out of it at will. But very few could I take in with me because of their unbelief in the presence of the kingdom here on earth now.

I moved to another church that called themselves full gospel. It seemed much better. The people there had experiences with God. They told others what God said. Most of the time it was word for word from the Bible but it was good to be among people who also claimed to hear from God. They didn’t take offense in me telling them that God told me this or that.

The members at this church even prayed for people for God to actually heal them. Sometimes it actually happened. But most of the time I got the impression that they didn’t really believe he would really answer prayer. I say this because they just kept asking for the same thing over and over as if God was hard of hearing. They just kept speaking like they thought that he would be more likely to hear them for their much speaking. Finally I asked God why they kept praying for the same thing over and over. To which the answer came to this and the other questions I hadn't yet asked.

"The prayer is spoken for the benefit of those around you. I know what my children have need of even before they ask? These people have known me yet they left their first love of me. Instead of coming back to me to be filled again and again they have chosen rather to stay out of my city and build their own. They lean on the flesh and listen to their own voice rather than hear from me. Even though they received me with joy, they have again become comfortable with their book. Rather than being rejected of men as you were they have formed a group that shares in the same ailment. They are content to find some agreement even as you were but they were satisfied to stop. Therefore, I have left them to their own devices and their eyes have been shut. In all their reaping shall they learn knowledge and shall come to the truth and their eyes will be opened and they will see again. I am not a cruel Father who punishes his children, as many would have you think. Is it cruel when you as a father allow your son whom has grown to make his own choices in life and reap the fruits of his actions? Is my love any less? Am I not with them all always? Some of them will hear the words I have given you and they will be encouraged and find me and continually seek me but they also will be rejected of this

very group they have made themselves a part of."

It wasn't long before I was at a prayer meeting and the pastor was feeling really good. God had lifted him up into his high places and the Pastor invited anyone to minister that wished. God spoke to me to go forward and I did. One woman was burdened because her uncle did not know God and she had been praying for him for years. Again I stepped into the city where the water was pure. My thoughts were one with the Father and as I opened my mouth I uttered. "Even as the Centurion told Jesus in Matthew 7:7 that he didn't need to go but just send his word, God's hand is touching your uncle this minute." The woman immediately fell out in the spirit as people in this church occasionally do. And as I was filled with joy and drunken with God's spirit, the Pastor came down from his high into his own thoughts and shut down the service. "This is not of God" he said. And shortly this was one more church that I was no longer welcomed at.

A week later, the woman who had been prayed for approached me to thank me for what was done. Her uncle in Spain had received God that selfsame hour. I was gone from the church now but not without explanation from the assistant pastor. He had approached me some time later and said that God does not work the way I did that day. He said "the Bible says how good are the feet of him that brings glad tidings of the Gospel. For how shall they be saved unless a preacher is sent? He will be saved when a preacher is sent. You don't even know if he has heard the gospel yet."

He was right in one way, I thought. I didn't know whether the man had heard the gospel yet. God knew. God was not limited and all I did was speak his words. Now I understood. They stumbled and were snared by a precept in the book. God was right; they loved the book and their own understanding more than the voice of the Spirit of God.

I was exhausting my choices in local churches. As long as I didn't speak I was welcome to sit and listen. I could sing along or read a passage in the Bible. If I were there long enough I could greet people and shake hands. I could volunteer my services in almost any area and they would be pleased. But only the pastor and a select few he had groomed could be used of God to expound on the things of God. To say anything new was to cross over the line. Most of the members I met seemed like such wonderful people. It was sad to watch them being manipulated this way by pastors they trusted. But how could I blame the pastors when the wonderful people would not think for themselves but instead agree to be willing victims. The pastors I met seemed to be thoughtful and friendly and caring. But in most all cases I found when they were cornered with truth, they chose rather to hold on to that which they had. It was then I would notice a quick change in their temperament as if truth were some sort of adversary.

Most that I met in these churches I found were comfortable with that which they had. Church attendance was high and most of the people were kept entertained by fine music and song. Sometimes it was so good that it would even bring tears to their eyes. Their faces were solemn during the preaching part most of the time but in song they seemed happy and free. They just don't get it I thought to myself feeling sad. Don't they want to hear God for themselves? What is it that they fear? And then it came to me. In the book of Exodus, on Mount Sinai, the people said to Moses, "*Speak thou with us, and we will hear: but let not God speak with us, lest we die.*" The people had turned away from him that speaks from heaven to have a go between on earth. It was the same today as it was then. The story wasn't talking about dying in the physical but rather dying to their old ways. These people did not want to give up the world of that which they had and were comfortable with. I felt so alone yet I was not alone. In God have I been persuaded to reside.

And God said, "*Be not saddened my son. For nothing is lost forever. All of creation is mine. A journey they are on for more than this one fleeting life. This time is but as a sand in the sea. In time they will tire through suffering and pain of their choosing until they chose that which should heal all their wounds."*

Yes, I said to myself. I will not be sad for them or myself. I will be content in that which I am given daily. I will not measure success in the abundance of things, which are but illusions of wealth. For all that is God's is mine for the asking yet I will be careful for that which I ask. There is no need to beg and plead to others to come. There is no need to use fear, intimidation or threats. What need does truth have of all these things? All will come to the Father in their own time.

Chapter 13
Meeting Herman

It was not long after I was rejected from that church that I met a man whose name was Herman. He was a bit younger than I was and was a strange looking red-headed man. I met him at a local revival and quickly was drawn to him. It was evident he had little education and lacked a fashion for dress. But when he opened his mouth it was even as if I was hearing my Father from within. Yet it came through his mouth. We sat for hours at a coffee shop sharing our thoughts with each other. There seemed to be nothing we couldn't say to each other. I heard things that I knew and things that yet were unknown to me. I didn't want to leave that place. At last I had found a friend who had similar words and understood the things that I had learned. We exchanged phone numbers and made plans to meet again at his place the next week. This was truly a gift from God, I thought.

As we met again and again we grew closer. Mutually we looked forward to our frequent visits. I knew because he told me so and we never lied to each other. It was like a mutual admiration society. We had the utmost respect for one another. It was a perfect relationship but I couldn't yet see what was happening to us.

We decided to work together and start a radio program. We would share that which God had showed us concerning his kingdom. Getting on radio was easy. The station didn't require credentials and as long as there were no obscene words there was no censoring. All they wanted was our money. Fifty dollars for a half-hour show. Once a week we would prepare our tape with conversations and no shortage of words. We both were emptying ourselves of that which we were given. There were no pastors to filter our words or ask us to leave. There was no one we had to please by diluting the truth. We were enjoying sharing God's message.

The money didn't matter to me for I had no vices to spend it on. And then one day it all came to an end. No, we didn't run out of money even though no one sent in donations but we did run out of words. Oh, we could have made some up but we knew what that would mean. After 13 weeks we packed up and left the Christian radio business.

Our Father had turned off the faucet and we both knew it. We had stayed out of the city and lived off old bread. Somehow through all of this we became so comfortable with each other that we did as others did before us. Even though there was only two of us, we were making our own church. We were neglecting our first love. We lived off our old bread that was good but for a day but failed to get a portion of fresh bread daily for ourselves. "Father", we cried, "Our eyes were almost shut. We grow thirsty again for the river of water that had stopped." Somehow, it loses its purity if it is not running. And so we cried out, "Flow it again unto us that our health might be restored."

"Now you have been made to understand about the narrow path. The nature of the spirit of the flesh sneaks back upon you. That which is illusion again becomes real before you. Like a ripple in the water it goes unnoticed till one no longer sees a true reflection of himself. To continue on your journey you must always watch for the deceitfulness of the spirits of the flesh. You must chose to reject them and stay on the course. Daily, you must look for me and connect with my spirit. To stop is to fall asleep again. You will go back if you do not go forward."

And with this Herman and I knew that our meeting was for a lesson to both of us. It was an encounter that was refreshing to the flesh but of little value to the spirit. It fed our need to be in agreement with others but at the expense of the new and fresh. After all, God is a living God and his thoughts stop not. We each must journey alone. Though we may pass in the breeze, we must remain focused on that which we seek lest we get back off-course ourselves. And so, we saw each other again from time to time and were thankful for our brief meetings but there was too much ahead for either of us to live in the past.

Each day was a new day and with it an encounter with God. Whether I heard him as audible voice or in deed or in thought or even just knew, it mattered little. In and out of his city I would go. I would take that which was given and share it in some way and my cup remained full.

Chapter 14
Truths

As I continued on my journey, it was plain to see that acceptance in the Christian Church system was not possible to one who places direct revelation over passed down teachings and the words in their Bible. Starting a new sect or denomination was also not the answer. It seemed all of the existing ones had only fragments of the truth and made it difficult to grow further. Once a new denomination was started its members also would force it into the same bondage. To continue on the journey there could be no room for religion. God had showed to me that religion says that there are THEY and WE. There are believers and non-believers, the saved and the lost, followers and infidels. Truth says that we are ALL children of the most high. There are no THEY and WE. There are only children somewhere on their journey.

Most religion as it is practiced has its associated story that must be believed. God had shown me that receiving truth is based on an openness to possibilities and a direct connection with Him. To me, religion and its associated story was not an openness to truth but rather man's vain attempt to define God on his own terms. And once defined, it is set in a concrete yoke whereby the believer willingly allows himself to be entangled. In essence the believer puts on self imposed invisible chains limiting his journey and travels to a defined plan. He locks himself to a narrow view and understanding of God, creation and truth.

To shed his shackles, man MUST BE WILLING to lay aside the traditions and teaching of man. Failure to do so and to be open to the new and different is the equivalence of believing that the world is flat and thus shutting out discovery. It is like putting blinders over our eyes and effectively stopping our progress on our journey.

Religion was not created by God to see God but rather by man to define God as he wants to see HIM. Truth is what one seeks by religion but for most there is an unwillingness to accept it directly and freely from God. Most prefer to have it defined for them by learned and educated men. Men educated in the past down doctrines of men. In the end these educated men will seek control over their proselytes. They will do this in what they believe and represent as the spirit of love.

Others prefer to work hard for truth as if they must

buy it to possess it. They read and study with fervor as if Truth has to be reasoned or figured out when in fact Truth just exists even as God himself does.

Much of my time henceforth was spent in the observation of people. It was not hard to see the cause of many people's unhappiness. The choice of which religion they practiced seemed to matter very little. The journey stops on many places and paths.

For many it was constantly living in the past. It seemed these people were always wishing things were like the way before this or that as if the past were a better time. Discontent with the present and moving on to greener pastures only to decide and believe that they were better off before. Focusing on the past and not looking where the path was leading and missing the present, no progress is apparent. In truth, nothing had really changed in their life. A man or woman can be about as happy as he or she will allow. This happiness is in spite of the circumstances. This requires that one must recognize NOW. There was always somebody around worse off than these people but I could not tell it by their attitude.

Then there are those who are well off but never satisfied. Their complex life brings them plenty of stress and anxiety yet they continually chose this more complex life over the simple things.They have determined that they must have more of what life has to offer. As a result they continually strive for more of what money can buy and the recognition that comes with it. They have not yet realized the truth that happiness is not in the abundance of what one has or in what other people think of you.

Some I noticed were constantly living in the future. They were dissatisfied with the past and the present and had resigned themselves to be full of misery and looking to the far off unseen world as their reward. A reward puffed up by their imaginations for the self-inflicted punishment that life was dealing them. This is the cup they have chosen. Their bed is made and no steps will be taken for now. Truth says we are free to be content and enjoy the present whatever it might be as we continue our journey through the NOW.

Then there are many people who are unhappy because their time is taken up believing that others are responsible for the sad state that they are in. Blaming their current condition and everything that happens to or doesn't happen to them on everyone else is at least for now their favorite pastime. Nothing is ever their fault. It is always what some other person does or says or doesn't do or say that is the problem. Truth says that we are responsible for our own actions and reactions. We have a choice whether we are offended or not. We have a choice in what we say or do in regards to inputs from others. These are not hard things to understand. Man is his own worst enemy in this matter. We believe a lie and reject the truth and are then held in bondage by our belief.

Others I saw were stuck in servitude to their lifestyle. Wanting to not deny themselves of material offerings, they live beyond their means. A life of servitude and bondage to a job, which many of them despise, is a bed they cannot yet find the strength to get up out of. Often, some of them resorted to risky gambles in hopes to break free. The answer to their dilemma lays in less and not more as a starting path to continue the journey.

Then I saw a large group of people on the journey who may not admit it but believe that all others should live up to the way they think people ought to. Hidden in their words and actions, they believe others don't look right, dress right, talk right, eat right, act right, smell right, vote right, believe right and in general conform to their standards. These seem to be the most unhappy group of people. Truth says their accusations and judgments have put themselves under a law that they themselves cannot live up to. It is no wonder that they are unhappy and unpleasant much of the time. They have fixated themselves on what they believe is the other persons problems and therefore stopped their own journey.

In truth, we all must pass by these stops. Some of us stay longer and many of us find ourselves often revisiting them long after we passed. One doesn't need a religion to see these things. One only needs an openness to possibilities and with that openness a connection with God and a love, understanding and forgiveness for self and all of mankind. And when one sees this he will not go around making laws for others and himself which is the yoke of bondage he creates. No, he will rather choose to live in peace and harmony with God and all of his creation which is his birthright as a child of the most high.

Truth can come as an awakening from within. It may be on a journey to the Holy Land. But it is not the physical place but rather a place that is lost in time and space. It is located nowhere and yet it is everywhere. It is that place we always wanted to go but in life seldom seem to get around to take the time to journey to. It is a city that cannot be seen with mortal eyes or where a focus exists for material things. Some call it New Jerusalem. Others may call it by some other name. It's name matters very little. Nevertheless, it exists.

To get there we must journey. It is a spiritual journey filled with many people. Yet, it is a journey that we all must go on alone. It has no detailed outlined written path. It's path is invisible to our fleshly eyes but when embraced directs us on from truth to truth constantly transforming our thoughts and mind; shedding our luggage and bringing us to God himself.

Chapter 15
The Conclusion

The days and the years have passed. It is now the year 2003. I am still an outcast among the people of the churches in whom I have had my part. I have seen some take hold of that which I have shared. Of course, those that do, in time they are also made not welcome. They must decide whether to go on or to turn back from where they came. And if they go on, among the churches they can no longer buy or sell that which they have received. They are treated as outcasts among the Christian churches and classified as lost souls headed to damnation. It is ironic in that it is recorded in their book that their Jesus was an outcast among the church of his day. Not much has changed. These outcasts have refused to accept the mark of the beast either in their mind or in their fellowship, which is the mark of a man. They follow not a man whose breath is in his nostrils. They walk in the Spirit of the living God. They do not buy The Story. Because of this, their own people must reject them even as Jesus was rejected by the church of his day.

The nature of the creature man has not changed. It remains as it was created in all men in the beginning. The question is whether we chose to follow that nature or seek a higher truth of that which created us and exists within each one of us. The masses continue to follow that which they are comfortable with. There is little more that we can do except to testify of the truth. Those that are ready and will hear... will hear. Those who will not hear... won't. In all of this we move on in our own journey. As men, our bed is made and we with blinders on continue to make gods of all that we see. And somehow there is wisdom in all this as we come full circle back to the face of our Father.

And I opened my mouth and cried out. "Father! Men say you are too busy to be a personal God involved in the details of life. They say you have better things to do. Some say that what happens here on earth or in one country is of little concern to you in this vast universe of universes. And some say men are just another group of creatures on earth who happen to be presently at the top of the food chain."

"And what do you say my son?"

"You are not a man that you can be too busy. You are neither male nor female. No flesh has seen your face. With flesh it is not possible to see that from which all is made. This is even as men cannot see their own thoughts with their eyes of flesh. We can only perceive your presence and be a part of your divine expression."

"You exist and live in all things that you have created. All this according to your good pleasure. You give life to that which you create. As long as life exists then you are there. Where there is movement, there is your breath."

"In your representation you have made us with the ability of thought and reason. Though we each live within our experience, you have given us the seed to see beyond. You have given us the ability to change and alter that, which is before us. You have created us with the ability to create and to destroy, to be in darkness or in light. You have put in our hands on this earth the ability or potential to subdue all other life unto ourselves. You have made us as gods in the earth."

"We have ourselves defined both right and wrong and good and bad. All things have you put before us, that we may chose, each having its own harvest. Your breadth is beyond our comprehension and no name can we attach to you."

www.ingramcontent.com/pod-product-compliance
Ingram Content Group UK Ltd.
Pitfield, Milton Keynes, MK11 3LW, UK
UKHW041846190726
13854UKWH00002B/737